# Enid Blyton's™
# ENCHANTED LANDS

# The
# Magician's Party

Hippo

Mollie and Peter have a big secret. The chair in their garden playroom is a Wishing Chair! Sometimes, it grows wings and whisks the children off on wonderful adventures! Mollie and Peter can't watch the chair all the time, but Jigs can. Jigs is their pixie friend who lives in the playroom. Whenever the chair grows its wings, Jigs runs to fetch them . . .

Scholastic Children's Books,
Commonwealth House, 1-19 New Oxford Street,
London WC1A 1NU, UK
a division of Scholastic Ltd

London ~ New York ~ Toronto ~ Sydney ~ Auckland

First published in the UK by Hippo, an imprint of Scholastic Ltd, 1998

Text Copyright © Abbey Communications Ltd, 1998
© Copyright in original stories and characters Enid Blyton Limited
Enid Blyton ™ Enid Blyton's signature is a registered Trade Mark of Enid Blyton Limited
Audio-visual series © Copyright Abbey Home Entertainment Limited, 1998
Licensed by PolyGram Licensing International.
Script adaptation by Caryn Jenner
Story consultant – Gillian Baverstock

ISBN 0 590 11348 8

Printed in Belgium

10 9 8 7 6 5 4 3 2 1

"Come and play, Jigs," called Mollie. "Please, Jigs," said Peter. "It's a rotten rainy day and we're bored!"

Outside the window, five little elves held up their umbrellas against the rain. But the children didn't notice the elves, because Jigs had arrived. He picked up three mugs from the table and began to juggle them.

"Careful, Jigs!" warned Mollie. Jigs flipped the mugs, and spun them round. Mollie and Peter clapped with delight.

Jigs tossed the mugs higher than ever. He was about to catch them, when there was a knock at the door. Jigs stumbled, and the mugs fell towards the floor!

"Jigs!" called Peter in a panic.

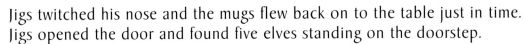

Jigs twitched his nose and the mugs flew back on to the table just in time. Jigs opened the door and found five elves standing on the doorstep.

  "Good evening, Jigs," they said all together. One by one, they entered the playroom and shook out their umbrellas, making Jigs dripping wet!
"Sorry about that, Jigs," they apologized.
"We've come to ask you if your Wishing Chair will take us to a party at Magician Greatheart's castle."

"May we come, too?" Jigs asked. "I've always wanted to meet Magician Greatheart."

"Yes, please!" the children piped up.

"It's a deal!" the elves replied. "You'll learn a lot from the Magician."

As Mollie, Peter, Jigs and the elves squeezed on, the Wishing Chair began to grow wings, as if it wanted to see the Magician too.

The Wishing Chair flew up through the clouds and rain. The raindrops turned to twinkling silver stars and the children saw a beautiful castle on top of a mountain.

A butler stood at the entrance to the castle to announce the guests.

"The elves," called out the butler.

"Welcome!" said Magician Greatheart. "I'm glad you've found your way here."

"The pixie, Jigs," called the butler.

"Magician Greatheart, I'm just dying to see your tricks!" said Jigs.

The Magician smiled. "You won't have long to wait."

"And the children," said the butler.

"Aha! Mollie and Peter!" said Magician Greatheart, as he shook their hands.

"How do you know who we are?" asked Mollie.

"Well, I am a magician!" he replied.

The entertainment at Magician Greatheart's party was amazing. There was a tumbler, a plate-spinner and a juggler who juggled even faster than Jigs!

Mollie, Peter and Jigs all cheered with the other guests.

Magician Greatheart flicked his finger and thumb, and a golden cane appeared in his hand. He tapped the cane on the ground, and a fountain of green smoke rose into the air.

The Magician tapped his cane again. The smoke disappeared and a shower of flowers scattered over the guests. Everyone cheered even more.

"Thank you all!" said Magician Greatheart. "Now, I'll put a spell on each of you so you can enjoy the party in exactly the way you'd most like."

Jigs chose first.

"I want to spend all night
being an entertainer!" he said.

"All night?" asked Magician
Greatheart. "Are you sure?"

"Oh, yes," said Jigs. "All night."

"As you wish!"

The Magician tapped his golden cane.
Immediately, four clubs appeared in
Jigs' hands, and he began to juggle.

Mollie and Peter wandered to the
dance floor. Mollie watched the
dancers wistfully.

"What is your wish?" Magician
Greatheart asked her.

"I want to dance all night in real silver shoes,"
Mollie declared.

"All night?" he asked. "Are you sure?"

"Oh yes," said Mollie. "All night."

Magician Greatheart tapped his golden cane. Mollie looked down to find that she was wearing beautiful silver shoes. A moment later, a handsome prince was at her side.

"Shall we dance?" he asked.

Mollie beamed, as she danced round the room with her prince.

Peter was eating a piece of cake offered by a waiter with a silver tray.

"Come, Peter," said the Magician. "The banquet awaits you."

The elves were already sitting quietly at the banquet table.

"What do you elves wish for this evening?" asked Magician Greatheart.

They all answered together. "We should each like one plate of tasty food and a glass of sparkling water, please."

The Magician tapped his cane. A plate of food and a glass of sparkling water appeared in front of each elf.

"Perfect. Thank you," they said.

"Peter? What would you like?" asked the Magician.
"I wish I could eat all night long," Peter answered.
"Then so you shall!" said the Magician.
He tapped his golden cane. All Peter's favourite foods suddenly appeared on the table.
"Great! Thanks!" he said, and he began to eat some of everything.

In the entertainment room, Jigs found himself twirling hoops, spinning plates and juggling, all at the same time! He was certainly a wonderful entertainer, but it was tiring work, and Jigs just wanted to have a rest. But he couldn't stop!

Mollie's head was whirling round fast as she whirled around the dance floor with one prince after another.

"Phew," she sighed, "I need to sit down now."

But as soon as one dance came to an end, another prince swept her off again.

Peter was still chomping his way through the food on the banquet table. Somehow, it didn't taste so delicious any more, and he had a huge tummy ache! But Peter couldn't seem to stop eating.

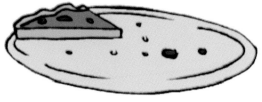

At the end of the party, Magician Greatheart said, "I trust you have all enjoyed yourselves in the way that you wished. I now release the spells."

He tapped his golden cane on the floor, and this time it disappeared.

Mollie could stop dancing at last.

"Oh, my poor feet!" she groaned.

She looked down and noticed that she was wearing her ordinary shoes again, but she didn't mind in the least.

Jigs dropped his hoops and plates and clubs, and wearily sank to the ground.
"Oh, I'm so tired," he sighed.
Peter put down his knife and fork. He held his stomach and moaned.
"Thank goodness," he said. "I couldn't eat another bite."
The elves were the only guests who were still cheerful.
"Splendid," they said. "Just right."

"One final piece of magic," said Magician Greatheart, smiling. He clicked his fingers, and the Wishing Chair appeared. The children, Jigs and the elves took their seats.

The Magician gave Mollie, Peter and Jigs one special egg each.

"These eggs are a small reminder of your visit. They will hatch when you arrive home."

"Thank you, Magician Greatheart," they said together. "Goodbye!"

"Have a safe journey," said the Magician as he waved goodbye.

21

The Wishing Chair flew
swiftly home.
 "Thank you for taking us
to the party," said the elves.
"We had a marvellous time!"
 "That's funny," said Peter.
"The elves really enjoyed
themselves."

 "Well, they weren't greedy like us," Mollie replied. "They didn't ask for
their wishes to last all night."
 "You can have too much of a good thing, you know," said the elves.
 Jigs gave a weary sigh. "You can say that again."
 "You can have too much of a good thing, you know," the elves
repeated. "Goodbye!"
 They shut the door quietly behind them.

"Hey," said Jigs, sitting up, "what about the Magician's eggs?"

They all pulled their eggs from their pockets. CRA-A-A-CK! CRA-A-A-CK! CRA-A-A-CK!

The eggshells cracked open.

Inside Mollie's egg was a colouring book and crayons. "Oh, good!" she said with a smile. "I can do this sitting down."

Peter had a puzzle. "This will keep me so busy I won't have a chance to think about food!" he laughed.

Jigs had a pack of cards. "I can learn some new tricks!" he said. Then he thought for a moment. "Maybe I'll build a house of cards instead."

"Let's not be greedy," said Mollie. "Let's just play these quiet games."

"The elves were right," said Peter. "You can learn a lot from Magician Greatheart."